The Lucky Cake

by Anna Prokos

illustrated by Christina Tsevis

a-to-z

publishing, llc

The Lucky Cake

Copyright © 2011 by Anna Prokos

Illustrated by: Christina Tsevis
Designed by: Patricia Dwyer

ISBN: 978-0-9838560-3-0 (paperback)
ISBN: 978-0-9838560-0-9 (hardcover)

Tell us about your lucky cake at:
theluckycakebook.com

For more kids' books from A-to-Z Publishing,
visit us at a-to-zpublishing.com

Printed in U.S.A.

Billy's favorite holiday finally arrived. "It's New Year's Day!" he cheered with excitement. "We get to eat Grandma's cake!"

Billy had waited all year for the special cake his yiayia
baked. It was soft, and round, and delicious. Best of all,
it held a shiny secret inside.

4

Yiayia placed the New Year's cake in the center of the table. A scrumptious smell filled the air. Billy's family hurried to set their eyes on the Vasilopita.

"It looks perfect!" Pappou told his wife, as he prepared to cut the holiday pita. He carefully held the knife over the center of the cake. "Who will get the lucky coin this year?"

Billy waited anxiously for his grandfather to make the first cut. He eyed the cake, hoping to spot the golden coin. But the flouri was nowhere to be seen.

Last year, Billy's brother Zac won the coin—and he had an awesome year! The year before, his brother Chris was the fortunate one. Billy was beginning to think he would never be lucky.

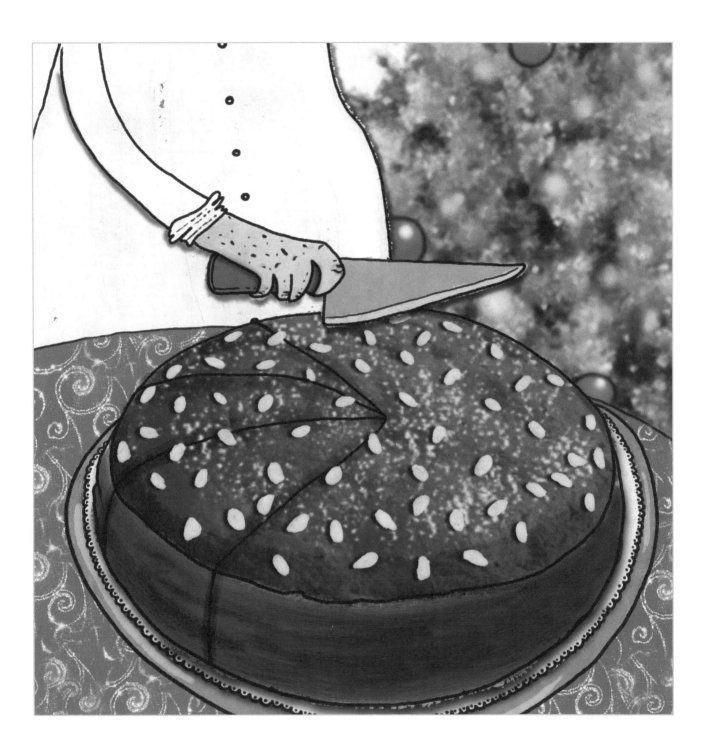

Pappou began by cutting three pieces. "This piece is for our church, the second slice is for our home, and the third piece is for Saint Basil," he said.

"Who's that?" Billy asked. "And why does he get our cake?"

"St. Basil the Great lived a long time ago," Pappou explained. "One day, a greedy ruler demanded that every villager give him their gold. He took their rings, and jewels, and coins.

"St. Basil felt sorry for the villagers. He begged and begged the ruler to give back their belongings. When he finally agreed, the ruler dumped all the treasure into St. Basil's arms.

"St. Basil didn't know who everything belonged to, so
he made a giant cake and put all the treasures into the
batter. He invited the villagers to church, where they
cut the cake together."

"The saying goes," Yiayia revealed, "that the villagers each found their own jewels in their piece of cake!"

"So to honor him, we bake a coin into the Vasilopita and we cut a piece for St. Basil," Pappou said.

Billy couldn't wait another second! "That's a great story, but can we please cut the Vasilopita? I've been waiting all year for this!"

Pappou winked and continued.

He cut the pieces in order from the oldest family member to the youngest. Pappou got the first piece and Yiayia got the next. Then, Billy's dad and mom, Zac, and Chris got their pieces of pita.

Finally, Pappou cut the final piece. "This slice goes to you, Billy, the youngest person in our family," he said with pride. "Enjoy!"

Billy bit into the wedge. Clink! His tooth hit something hard. A shiny speck glittered through the crumbs. "I got the coin! I got the coin!" Billy shouted.

Everyone gathered around Billy to see the golden
New Year's coin. The whole family hugged him and
kissed him on both cheeks. They were especially
happy for him.

"I wish you a healthy and happy new year, Billy!"
Pappou said.

"Don't forget lucky, Pappou!" Billy said.

"Oh, Billy," laughed his grandfather. "Do you think you
need a coin for luck? Just look around you."

Billy looked over at the dining room table. All the people he loved were happily gathered together, sharing stories and eating their delicious lucky cake.

"You're right, Pappou! I am the luckiest kid in the world."
He paused for a moment. "But just to be safe—" Billy
slipped the coin safely into his pocket.

Then, he took another bite of his Vasilopita.
"I can tell," Billy said, as he licked his lips,
"I am going to have a very lucky year!"

Our Family's Vasilopita Recipe

What You Need:

1 cup (2 sticks) unsalted butter, softened

1 cup sugar

3 extra-large eggs

4 cups flour

1 cup milk

Grated rind of 2 oranges

3 teaspoons vanilla extract

2 teaspoons baking powder

½ teaspoon salt

1 egg yolk, whisked

¼ cup sesame seeds

¼ cup blanched almonds

 a flouri, or a clean coin wrapped in foil

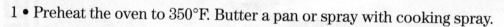

What You Do:

1 • Preheat the oven to 350°F. Butter a pan or spray with cooking spray.

2 • In a large bowl, cream the butter until it is light and fluffy. Add the sugar and beat for one minute.

3 • Slowly beat in the eggs, one at a time. Fold in the orange zest.

4 • In a separate bowl, sift together the flour, baking powder, and salt.

5 • With the mixer on low speed, gradually beat in the flour mixture alternating with the milk. If the mixture is very thick, use a wooden spoon to blend in the remaining flour. Beat until smooth.

6 • Spread the batter into the pan and drop the coin into the batter. Don't let anyone see where you place it! Make sure the coin is completely covered with the batter.

7 • Brush the top evenly with the whisked egg and sprinkle with sesame seeds. Gently press the blanched almonds into the top to make a design. The date of the new year is traditional.

8 • Bake for 45 minutes, or until golden brown. Cover with foil if it browns too quickly. Cool in the pan for 15 minutes before removing. Cut the cake when it has completely cooled to room temperature.

* In some families, it is customary for the winner of the coin to receive money or a prize from the senior member of the family. What will your tradition be?

About Billy

Billy knows he is a lucky kid, but he wants to carry around his coin anyway! In Greek, Billy's name is Vasilios (vah-SEE-lee-os), which is the Greek name for Basil. That's why St. Basil's cake is called Vasilopita. (va-see-LO-pee-tah). Many Greek boys who are named Vasilios or girls who are named Vasiliki are named after St. Basil. They celebrate their name day on January 1—the same day St. Basil is honored with a Vasilopita. Billy is going to have a great year thanks to his lucky coin. He can't wait to share his adventures in his next book, *The Lucky Year*.

About the Author

Anna Prokos cherishes the three lucky coins she has won over the years from her mom's Vasilopita. Sometimes, she tucks one in her pocket just for good luck. The Greek-American author has written a number of books and magazine articles for children. This is her first book published by A-to-Z Publishing, a children's media company she founded in 2008. Ms. Prokos live in Bergen County, NJ, where she and her family spend hours exploring libraries, bookstores, and other adventurous places.

About the Illustrator

Christina Tsevis believes she expresses herself best through her illustrations. She was raised in a very artistic environment, and has been creating her unique designs since she was a teen. Music and animals inspire this artist to create works of art that usually feature children set in complex and symbolic backgrounds. Ms. Tsevis lives in Athens, Greece, where she enjoys hiking uphill and taking in the view of ancient monuments and blue seas.

About A-to-Z Publishing

At A-to-Z Publishing, LLC, we specialize in books that help children be and achieve their best. Anna Prokos, a respected author of over 40 children's books, founded the company in 2008, and now we're growing with our readers, publishing books and e-books designed to inspire, educate, and motivate children to explore their world and spark curiosity in their minds and hearts. The A-to-Z staff has a combined 30 years experience with publishers such as Sesame Workshop, Scholastic, Time for Kids, MAD Magazine, Discovery Channel School, and others. We use this experience and collective passion to help kids live, do, and be well.

a-to-z
publishing, llc

Anna Prokos, founder
Patricia Dwyer, designer
Valentina Palladino, intern/assistant

With many thanks to my family, especially Yianni, Zachary, Christopher, and William.
I am the luckiest person in the world! —AP

Printed in the USA
CPSIA information can be obtained
at www.ICGtesting.com
LVHW061141240124
769488LV00007B/155